CAMPAIGN CHAOS!

rhcbooks.com

ISBN 978-1-5247-7291-8 (trade) — ISBN 978-1-9848-5148-2 (lib. bdg.)

Printed in the United States of America

10 9 8 7 6 5 4 3 2

CAMPAIGN CHAOS!

BY MOLLIE FREILICH

Random House New York

I was sitting on my bed, moments away from diving into my latest *Muscle Fish* comic book, when I heard the static buzz of my walkie-talkie.

"Lincoln! *Lincoln!* Come in, Lincoln! Do you read me?" It was my best friend, Clyde McBride, shouting frantically. He clearly had something he needed to share with me. Maybe he'd seen a ghost and needed the help of a fellow *ARGGH!* cadet to catch it. Or maybe an alien had just landed in his yard, and he wanted me there to make first contact. Or maybe his dads had made their famous guacamole, and they needed a taste tester. Or maybe . . .

"*LINCOLN! Ahhhh!*" I tumbled off the bed and fell in a heap on the floor. I scrambled to grab my walkie-talkie.

"Sorry, Clyde! I'm here! I read you loud and clear, buddy. Over," I replied.

"Lincoln! *Phew!* I was worried I'd have to call your house and Lori would answer the phone and I'd faint and forget what I had to say and—"

"*CLYDE!* Get ahold of yourself!" Clyde has a little crush on my oldest sister, Lori, and tends to spin out of control when he starts talking about her or to her.

"Thanks, pal. I needed that. Listen, this is big news. *Really* big news. I think I'd better tell you in person. Can I come over? Over." The suspense was almost unbearable, but I figured I could wait a few more minutes. Clyde hadn't been this excited to tell me something since the school cafeteria added rosemary to their meatloaf.

"Sounds like a plan," I said. "I'll meet you outside. Over and out."

My brain was racing a mile a minute trying to figure out what Clyde was going to say. I nearly tripped over my baby sister, Lily, as I sprang from my room to dash downstairs.

"Sorry, Lil!" I called over my shoulder as my infant sister stuck out her tongue to blow a raspberry at me.

I sprinted down the seemingly empty hallway, aiming for the stairs. I was nearly at the bannister when the high-pitched *screeeeeeech* of a whistle made me skid to a stop. My six-year-old twin sisters, Lola and Lana, decked out in matching aviator sunglasses and neon orange sashes, stood before me. I guessed they were practicing their hall-monitor duties at home again.

"What did we tell you about running in the halls?" Lana asked me, tilting her sunglasses down to give me a stern look.

"C'mon, guys! I have to get downstairs. Clyde will be here in a few minutes."

"Answer the question or we'll toss you in the clink!" Lola shouted, pointing at a cardboard box with bars cut out to resemble a jail cell. I knew they were serious. They once locked our sister Luan up just for telling bad jokes! Come to think of it, I'm surprised she isn't in there more often.

"Okay, okay. I promise I'll slow my pace down to a brisk walk." I sighed, eyeing the staircase.

Lola scratched some words on a notepad, then ripped off a piece of paper and handed it to me. "Consider this your last warning, Linky. Now move it! We have a hallway to patrol."

They both folded their arms and glared at me. I walked as quickly as I could to the top of the stairway. Once I was out of the twins' line of sight, I darted down the stairs, clinging to the railing for balance. I jumped over Lynn's skates; dodged Luan's ventriloquist dummy, Mr. Coconuts; and narrowly avoided Luna's amp. With a family this big, you usually have to navigate through some clutter.

Finally, I reached the front door, just in time to hear the sweet squeak of Clyde's yellow tandem bicycle rolling up in front of my house. I flung the door open and whirled outside to greet him.

"Clyde!" I called as I jogged down our front steps. Clyde was breathing heavily, like he'd just peddled the bike while hauling a grand piano behind him. "Are you okay?"

"Just." *Gasp.* "Need." *Gasp.* "A." *Gasp.* "Second," he puffed out as he removed his helmet and sat down on the lawn. It felt like a million years passed, but finally, he was able to speak again. "I'm going to do it. I'm going to run for school treasurer."

"That's amazing, Clyde!" I said as I gave him a high five. This was *huge* news! Clyde was scared of speaking in front of big crowds, becoming popular, *and* watching someone else's piggy bank, so if he ran for treasurer, he'd have to overcome three of his fears. "Let's go inside and celebrate with some ice-cold lemonade."

We sat at my dining room table, sipping our delicious drinks left over from my sister Lola's lemonade stand.

"So, why do you want to be treasurer, anyway?" I asked, avoiding bringing up his many running-for-treasurer-related fears.

"My therapist, Dr. Lopez, keeps telling me it

would be good for me to try something new and push my boundaries. So when they announced at school yesterday that sign-ups were due for student council elections, I panicked, closed my eyes, and wrote my name down on the sheet. Then I opened my eyes and saw I'd signed up to be treasurer. There's only one teensy little problem." Now that he had fully caught his breath, Clyde was talking a mile a minute.

"What's that?"

"Lincoln, I'll be honest with you. I'm not exactly sure what a treasurer does." He sighed and put his head down on the table, looking defeated.

"Don't worry, Clyde. A treasurer . . ." I scratched my head. "A treasurer is . . . A treasurer does . . ." Dang it. I had no idea. I couldn't help my best friend.

"A treasurer is responsible for the school's fiscal accountability and financial stability."

Clyde and I turned our heads toward the voice. It was my sister Lisa. She might be only four years old, but she was easily the smartest person I knew. If anyone could help us figure out what Clyde was running for, it would be her.

"The school's what and what?" I asked.

Lisa sighed. "A treasurer takes care of the student council's money. They track the budget, plan activities for the students, and help raise funds for things around the school."

"Like school dances? Or new volleyball nets for the gym? They do need new nets after that incident with the fencing club," Clyde said to Lisa.

"Precisely," she responded, adjusting her glasses.

"Oooh," Clyde and I said together.

"Now, if you'll excuse me, I have to run a brain wave test on Lana while she makes mud pies. I believe the mere act of handling soil excites her brain synapses and creates serotonin." Clyde and I stared at her blankly. Sometimes it was hard to understand what Lisa said. She sighed and explained, "It makes her happy to play with dirt." *Ah.*

Lisa left the dining room to go upstairs. Clyde's eyes went wide. His palms were sweating. He had the look of a kid who just realized he was onstage at the spelling bee in his underwear.

"Clyde, what's wrong?" I asked.

"This is a bad idea. What if the other kids make fun of me for running for treasurer? What if I don't get a single vote? What if I go up to give my speech and my shirt is on inside out? What if I have to run against one of our friends? What if my only competition is a really cute pug puppy? What if I can't actually count? I did get a B-plus on that last math test, after all. What if aliens come down and take over my body, and then they become the school treasurer and then—"

"CLYDE!" I shouted. He paused and looked at me. "You're spiraling."

"I just don't think I can do this," he said sadly. He dropped his head into his hands. I couldn't stand to see my best buddy in the whole wide world feel this bad.

"Remember when we went to Dairyland Amoosement Park and we were finally tall enough for the Butter Beater roller coaster?"

"Yeah, but—"

"Remember how scared we both were? And how we waited in line for four whole hours?"

"Yeah, but—"

"When we finally got to the front of the line, you were the one who said, 'Lincoln, it's now or never.' I don't think I would've gone on that roller coaster without you. You knew that if we didn't ride it right then, we'd never ever get on it. You knew that it was perfectly safe and built to be fun. And then what happened?"

"We had the best time."

"We had the *best* time. We rode it again and again! We didn't get to go on any other rides because we only rode the Butter Beater! It was great!"

Clyde smiled. "You're right, Lincoln," he said. "But what does that have to do with running for treasurer?"

"You have the perfect attitude for student council, Clyde. You care about other people, you care about Royal Woods Elementary School more than anyone I know, and you're the kind of person who understands when it's time to get on the roller coaster."

"Thanks, pal. I appreciate your support. Now, I have a very important question to ask you," he said seriously. "But I will totally understand if you say no."

"You're my best friend. You can ask me anything."

"Lincoln, you're the man with the plan," he said as he reached into his backpack and pulled out a clipboard with a big red bow attached. "Will you be my campaign manager?"

I've coached Lola and Lana for pageants. I've been Luan's right-hand clown. I helped

Leni learn how to drive. I was sure I could be a campaign manager. How hard could it be, anyway?

"Clyde, it would be my honor," I said, going down on one knee like a knight from a medieval movie.

Clyde laughed. "Arise, Sir Lincoln, Knight of the Campaign Table!" he said in a thick British accent like the king in *King of the Rings* as he tapped each of my shoulders in turn with a pencil. I got up and took the clipboard from him.

"Operation Help Clyde Run for School Treasurer is a go!" We bumped fists and did our best-friend handshake. "Let's get started!"

Clyde and I approached the campaign as we would have any other school project: with craft supplies and a plan. As campaign manager, I decided our first order of business was to make posters. When you ran for student council, Principal Huggins let you hang up as many posters as you wanted, as long as they weren't mean-spirited toward the other candidates and didn't cover up anyone else's poster (or anything important, like a fire alarm). With that in mind, Clyde's dads, Harold and Howard, took us on an awesome poster supply shopping spree so we'd be able to make a bunch of posters.

We went to Arts 'N' Things, the craft supply store at the Royal Woods Mall, and filled up two whole shopping carts with poster board, crayons, bright paint, paintbrushes, and glitter. The glitter was Clyde's idea. He said it would make his posters stand out. The Arts 'N' Things employee at the register was really nice and wished Clyde good luck with his campaign.

Clyde's dads helped us carry our stuff into their house.

"If you need any help at all, let us know," Howard said as he finished laying down newspaper in the living room so we could paint.

"You know, Howie ran for student council in college," Harold mused as he put down the last bag.

"My dad was elected vice president!" Clyde told me proudly.

"Wow, Mr. McBride! Did you have the most posters? Did you have the best speech? Were you the most popular?" I had so many questions for Clyde's dad. I was determined to be the best campaign manager possible. I couldn't let my best friend down—he had to win! Both of Clyde's dads laughed.

"Come to think of it, I didn't have the most posters, and I wasn't very popular," Howard said. "But I will tell you this: I was always the most *me* I could be. I never tried to be anyone other than myself. I think people liked that

I was just Howard."

"And you were very honest. Honesty goes a long way," Harold added, "especially for a politician." They both laughed. Clyde and I shrugged. Adult jokes, I guess.

"Thanks for the tips," I said. I already had so many ideas for posters jumping around in my head, and I could tell Clyde did, too. We were eager to get started. "I think we've got this. Clyde's going to be the best treasurer Royal Woods Elementary has ever seen."

"Good luck, fellas! We'll get out of your hair," Howard said as he and Harold left the room. It was time to start brainstorming poster slogans.

Clyde and I had been best friends since we were really little. We had a lot of things in common, we worked well together, and we never fought. Together, we were Clincoln McLoud. We could do anything! As Clyde's campaign manager, it was my duty to get things started.

"Lisa said school treasurers are responsible for money. Maybe we should make posters that highlight your math skills," I suggested as I pulled a piece of poster board in front of me.

"That's a great idea, Lincoln! Maybe we can come up with some memorable slogans. People love a memorable slogan."

"Yes! Good call, Clyde!" But what? What would make people remember Clyde while also making them think he was the best candidate?

Clyde furrowed his brow. I could tell he was thinking really hard. Then, suddenly, he snapped his fingers.

"I've got one! 'Vote for Clyde! It just

makes *cents*!' But instead of spelling *sense* as S-E-N-S-E, we spell it like money: C-E-N-T-S!"

"You're a genius, buddy!" I wrote down his idea on a piece of paper. "Oh, I've got one!"

"I'm all ears."

"How about 'Clyde can count, so count on Clyde'?"

"Yes! That's great! Add it to the list!"

I scribbled down my idea. Suddenly, another idea burst into my brain.

"What if we cut up a picture of you and put plus signs in between? Like legs plus arms plus head plus body? And then the caption could be 'It all adds up to a perfect candidate. Vote Clyde for Treasurer!'"

"Yes!" Clyde exclaimed. "Though we should probably find a good picture to use for that, like one where my eyes are open. I don't want to revisit the fourth-grade yearbook situation," he said. We both shuddered. In Clyde's fourth-grade yearbook picture, one of his eyes was closed, and the flash left a weird mark on his face, so he looked kind of like a mean, sleepy pirate. It was not his best look.

"These are great," I said.

"I've got another one!" Clyde exclaimed excitedly. "What about something like 'Bank on me, and I'll treasure your vote'?"

I added his idea to our list, but my eyebrows rose. "I think you've been catching too many of Luan's comedy shows," I said. My sister Luan is the master of puns, and Clyde's suggestion seemed a lot like something she'd say.

"Have you heard her latest joke about the rhinoceros and the dentist? It's just too funny!"

"What about the rhinoceros—" I stopped myself. "We have to focus, Clyde!"

We continued brainstorming for another hour. The whole paper was covered in slogan ideas. Then, slowly but surely, we started making Clyde's posters. First, we penciled the outlines of the letters. When we were sure everything was spelled right, we filled in the letters with paint.

We worked for hours. I could barely feel my fingers after painting for so long. Clyde's cats, Cleopawtra and Nepurrtiti, were curled up on the couch, sleeping. Even *they* were tired of us making posters.

It felt like forever! Finally, just after dinner but with time to spare before bed, we were done. We had made thirty posters completely by hand. Exhausted but proud, Clyde and I high-fived. Then Lori picked me up in Vanzilla, our family van, and took me home.

The next morning, Clyde and I got to school early to hang up his posters.

"It's important that every single kid is able to see your posters," I said as I rolled out a map I had drawn of our school. I had marked a bunch of places on campus with big red X's. "If we put them in the places where I've drawn an X, we should be covered."

Clyde looked over my work.

"Wow, Lincoln. You have completely covered all the major landmarks: the lockers right next to the nurse's office, that bulletin board outside the gym, the doors to the music room, and even the blank wall in the hallway outside the cafeteria, where the floor is permanently sticky. There's no way anyone will miss these," he said with a grin.

"Right? Okay, I think it's best if we split up and each go to half of the school. How about you take the south side, where the good water fountains and the chemistry lab are," I said as I pointed to places on the map, "and I'll take the north side over by the trophy case and the best door to catch the bus. Once we've put all these up, we can meet outside Principal Huggins's office and check the list of candidates to see who you're running against."

"Sounds like a plan!"

"We've got this!"

"Thanks again, Lincoln."

"No sweat, buddy. Maybe when you're

treasurer, you can get the librarian to buy that book about writing comics."

"The one by Bill Buck, creator of Ace Savvy and One-Eyed Jack, the greatest heroes of all time?"

"Yeah, that one! Every time I try to check it out at the Royal Woods Main Library, someone else already has it. I asked the school librarian if she had a copy, and she said it's on their list of books to buy, but they don't have the funds right now. Maybe she could use the help of Super School Treasurer Clyde McBride!"

As soon as I said that, it was as if a light bulb had sprung from Clyde's head.

"I've got it!"

"You've got what?" I asked, totally clueless.

"What if I go around and ask students and teachers what they think the school needs?

Then I'll have a better understanding of how I can help them if I become treasurer."

"Clyde, that's genius! But first"—I pointed at our stack of posters—"let's get these all up."

I walked down the hall with a spring in my step. I found every nook and cranny from my map and expertly attached the posters with school-approved tape. I couldn't wait for our other friends to see our handiwork. I hadn't been this proud of an arts and crafts project since the family diorama I made—but accidentally broke—of me and all ten of my sisters.

I hung the last of my batch of posters outside the teachers' lounge and headed toward Principal Huggins's office to meet up with

Clyde. It was getting closer to the start of the school day, so kids were starting to trickle in through the doors. I saw some of them giggling and nodding at one of our posters. This one had a picture of Clyde dressed as an owl and the caption "It's wise to vote for Clyde—'Owl' be the best choice!" This was another of pun-loving Luan's suggestions. We'd been running out of ideas, so we went with it.

When I finally got to the bench outside the principal's office, Clyde was already there waiting for me. He was waving and smiling at all the passing students. My usually pretty shy best friend was *actually* greeting kids he didn't know. I was so impressed.

I gave Clyde a high five. "Operation Put Posters Up on the North Side of School is officially complete."

He gave me another high five. "South side is all done, too!"

A group of our friends—Rusty, Stella, Liam, and Zach—came up to where we were talking.

"Hey, Clyde!" Rusty hollered as they all approached. "You're running for treasurer? That's awesome, man! You definitely have my vote."

"Y'all got my vote, on accounta all that glitter," Liam piped in. "My meemaw never let me use it, on accounta it scarin' the chickens." Liam lived on a farm and got to be around all sorts of animals.

"Your posters are really clever, Clyde. I love a good counting pun. We didn't have student council at my last school," Stella said.

"Thanks, everyone! I really appreciate your support," Clyde said, smiling.

We all looked at Zach, who hadn't said anything.

"What?" he asked. "I don't vote. My parents told me not to trust any bodies of government."

"Zach, Clyde's running for student council, not to be the governor of Michigan," Stella said, rolling her eyes.

"Yeah. For now," Zach whispered. We looked at him sideways. Zach was really into conspiracy theories about the government. There'd be no changing his mind.

"See, Clyde? That's already five votes, including yours and mine," I said.

"Lincoln, I think there might be a chance I could win this thing. People seem to like my posters, and Dr. Lopez was right—I feel more confident already! I feel sorry for the poor chump who runs against me," Clyde said as he theatrically puffed out his chest.

"Clyde," I said softly.

"Why, that poor kid doesn't know what's coming," he said even louder, moving his hands through the air as if he was making a grand speech.

"Clyde."

"I'm going to sweep this election! Not a single vote will go to that other kid! Even *they* will vote for me!" he shouted, jumping on top of the bench.

"CLYDE!"

He stopped.

"Whoa. Sorry, buddy. I think I got a little out of hand with that whole confidence thing."

"It's not that, Clyde. Look," I said, pointing at the list Principal Huggins's secretary had just pinned to the bulletin board outside the office.

"Is that the list of candidates?" Clyde asked.

"Looks like it," Rusty said, reading the piece of paper.

"Wee-ooo!" Liam exclaimed. "Good luck, friend! Looks like you're running against Chandler."

Clyde and I both froze. *Chandler? Why'd it have to be Chandler?* Chandler is this kid who's kind of mean but super popular because he throws this huge birthday party at the sewage treatment plant every year. It's the coolest party and everyone wants to go, but not everyone gets invited. Last year, Clyde and I tried really hard to get invited—we almost cost Lori her waitressing job at Gus's Games and Grub—but we didn't make the cut.

"Don't freak out, guys. Chandler's posters are pretty basic and old-school. I saw one over by my locker. They're just pictures of his face," Stella assured us.

Clyde and I breathed a sigh of relief.

"We should get to class. You guys coming?" Rusty asked.

"Clyde and I will meet you there," I replied. "We've gotta check out Chandler's posters first."

Our friends waved goodbye and walked down the hall to Mrs. Johnson's classroom. Clyde looked a little worried. I was worried, too. Beating Chandler was going to be tough.

Clyde and I were walking down the hall to find one of Chandler's posters—it seemed like he'd made less than a quarter of the number of posters Clyde and I had made—when we saw the first plunger. Girl Jordan was at her locker, holding a plunger with *Chandler 4*

Treasurer written boldly across the suction cup part in one hand and a giant novelty lollipop with Chandler's face drawn on it in sugar in the other. Clyde and I were speechless. Our jaws dropped to the floor.

"Hey, Girl Jordan," I said timidly.

"Oh, hi, Lincoln," she said. "Can you hold this?" She handed me the plunger. Lana is basically a professional plumber, and she's tried to teach me over the years about the gadgets she uses. This was no flimsy piece of equipment. This was a top-of-the-line toilet tool. Girl Jordan opened her locker and took the plunger from my hand.

"So, um, where'd you get those?"

"Chandler's giving them out outside by the picnic tables! The lollipops are cherry, which is my favorite flavor, so I think I'm definitely going to vote for him."

Clyde hadn't moved since we ran into Girl Jordan. He looked like he'd seen a ghost. I was afraid he might pass out. Girl Jordan looked at Clyde with concern.

"Is he okay?" she asked, pointing at Clyde.

"I think so," I said.

"*Ooo*okay. See you in class," she said, practically skipping down the hallway with the lollipop.

Clyde still hadn't moved. I grabbed him by the shoulders and shook him lightly.

"*AH!* Lincoln! What are we going to do?" he cried as another two kids with plungers and lollipops passed by.

"Don't worry, buddy. I have a plan."

I did not have a plan . . . yet. I knew I couldn't let Clyde down as his campaign manager, but I had no idea how to compete with plungers and lollipops. Clyde was so nervous, he was on the verge of collapsing.

"Clyde, don't worry, I've got this," I said, trying to convince myself as much as I was trying to convince Clyde.

"Lincoln, there were plungers. So many plungers."

"It'll be okay. Just head to Mrs. Johnson's class. I'll be right behind you. I have to do some last-minute campaign stuff."

Clyde still looked unsure, but I flashed him a big smile, trying to assure him that I knew what I was doing. He shrugged and smiled back.

"You're right. It's all going to be okay. Thanks, Lincoln."

I gave him a thumbs-up. "We've got this!"

Clyde walked toward our classroom. As soon as he was out of sight, I panicked. I had to come up with something! I started rummaging through my pockets and my backpack, trying to find anything of value I could part with on

Clyde's behalf. As kids passed by me on the way to class, I handed them whatever I had, hoping that would convince them to vote for Clyde.

"Here, Joy, have my last stick of gum! And don't forget to vote for Clyde McBride for treasurer!"

Joy stared at me like I had a booger stuck to my face.

"Hey, Ken, you look like you could use another shoelace! Here, take my extra! Vote for Clyde!"

Ken almost tripped over a trash can in confusion over my attempted gift.

"Sammie! What's happening? How would you like a token for Gus's Games and Grub? Here! Take it! Clyde McBride, future treasurer, would want you to have it."

Sammie grabbed the token from my hand

and ran away from me at lightning speed.

I went on and on, giving away every single thing I could, until all I had left was one of Lily's socks (I don't know how that got in my backpack) and a dust bunny shaped like the head of famed weatherman Patchy Drizzle, but no one wanted either of those. I glanced at the clock on the wall. It was almost time for class. I'd have to come up with other ideas to make Clyde stand out from Chandler.

As I sped past the band room and the trophy case on my way to Mrs. Johnson's classroom, it came to me: What if I gave Clyde a parade? People *loved* parades! Parades were even better than plungers. I got to Mrs. Johnson's room, slipped through the door, and sat at my desk just as the final bell rang.

After a lesson about measuring the volume

of a cylinder, it was finally lunchtime. Clyde still looked pretty upset about how things were going so far with his campaign, but I was determined to lift his spirits. Now all I needed was a band for my parade.

The problem was that our school marching band was already at a parade. It was their annual day at Dairyland Amoosement Park. Every year, they get to march down the middle of the park playing the Dairyland theme song. When they're done, they get to spend the rest of the day at the park just goofing off. *Hmm, maybe I should join band. . . .*

Without a band, I couldn't have a parade. *Wait!* I snapped my fingers. *I got it!* Clyde and I once tried to go through a huge to-do list of fun things on our spring break, but because we only had one day to do it, we had to split the list up. "Have a jam session" was on my list, so I built a one-man-band suit. I just had to suit up and become a one-man *marching* band!

Clyde and I were walking to our lockers to get our lunches. He'd probably try to stop me if I told him about my parade idea—he'd think it was too much attention, and he's not much of an attention guy—so I'd have to tell a little lie to get out of having lunch with him. I didn't *want* to lie to my best friend, but I *had* to!

"Oooh, Clyde," I groaned, clutching my stomach. "I think I—*burp*—need to go to the nurse. I'm feeling queasy." It was a terrible lie, but it was the best I could come up with on short notice.

"Let me take you," Clyde said.

"No, don't worry. You go to the cafeteria, and I'll take myself to the nurse's office."

"I couldn't let you go alone!"

"I—I . . . umm . . . I might have to stop at the bathroom on the way there, and I don't want you to have to . . . umm . . . wait for me and get worried," I said, trying my hardest to keep my "sick" face going.

"Oh no! What if the stress of my campaign is what's making you feel sick? What if I'm the cause of your ailment? And on top of that, I can't even get you the help you need! What kind of friend am I?"

"I have to go!" I shouted. In a panic, I ran as fast as I could away from Clyde. "Don't follow me!" I called as I turned the corner.

It wasn't my best move—and in the moment, it didn't make me feel like a great friend—but I knew it would be worth it once I was marching down the hall. Clyde would understand. And he'd forgive me for lying. At least, I hoped he would. I ducked into the band room and looked around. There were a few instruments out. If my super musically talented older sister Luna were here, she'd know which ones I should play and which ones would sound weird together. But I didn't have time to ask or figure that out. It was time for Operation Become a One-Man Band, and I was ready!

I tightened the bass drum strap, adjusted the neck holder for the harmonica, fixed the wrist straps for the cymbals, taped the trumpet to my forearm, and hugged the bagpipes under my armpit. The end-of-lunch bell was about to ring, and soon the hallways would be filled with kids going to class. It would be the perfect time to celebrate my buddy. I took a deep breath and stepped out into the hall.

*BOOM BOOM BOOM! Craaashhh!
Craaashhh! HONK HONK! Blurrrrrp!
Wheeeeeeeeeeeze!* I made my way down the
hallway, smiling my biggest smile and pounding
away at my instruments. I'd attached one of
Clyde's posters to my back to show people why
I was parading down the halls.

*BOOM BOOM BOOM! Craaashhh!
Craaashhh! HONK HONK! Blurrrrrp!
Wheeeeeeeeeeeeze!* There was just one tiny
problem with my band: I didn't really know
how to play any of the instruments. Every kid
I passed covered their ears. Students who were
usually the last to get to class were running past
each other to be the first.

"Move it! I need to get away from this
racket!" I heard one kid shout as he jetted past
a group of first graders.

BOOM BOOM BOOM! Craaashhh! Craaashhh! HONK HONK! Blurrrrrp! Wheeeeeeeeeeeze!

"UGH! It sounds like a duck pretending to be a cat pretending to be a cow!" a third grader cried as she rushed past me.

BOOM BOOM BOOM! Craaashhh! Craaashhh! HONK HONK! Blurrrrrp! Wheeeeeeeeeeeze!

"I'd rather have three weeks of detention than listen to this noise!" someone yelled.

BOOM BOOM BOOM! Craaashhh! Craaashhh! HONK HONK! Blurrrrrp! Wheeeeeeeeeeeze!

"I know who I *won't* be voting for! That Clyde guy!" another kid howled as he ran into a classroom.

The hallway was empty. Everyone had run to

their classrooms, even though the bell was still minutes away from ringing.

I stopped playing.

I stopped marching.

Suddenly, I felt really bad. This was not the plan. Instead of helping Clyde's campaign, I'd hurt it. I'd have to fix it somehow. I returned the instruments to the band room and hoped Clyde wouldn't hear about my unsuccessful attempt to get people to vote for him.

I had to shake it off and come up with another plan.

As I walked to my locker, I passed a sign-up sheet for the drama club. Immediately, another idea popped into my head: What if I put on a play? It would show everyone how Clyde would improve the school if he was elected. There wasn't enough time to write a script, get a cast, rehearse, and perform a whole play before the elections. After all, the elections were only a week away. I'd have to speed up the theater process a little bit.

I created a makeshift stage on top of one of the picnic tables in the schoolyard. I borrowed a big, puffy Shakespeare shirt and velvet feathered hat from the drama club's costume closet and a spotlight from the audiovisual club. I waited for the final school bell to ring. *When it rings, everyone will come flying outside. When they see me onstage, they'll definitely stop to watch,* I thought.

Brrrrrrrrrrrrrrrrrrrrrrrinnnnnnnnnng! The final bell blasted from the speakers. I cleared my throat and readied myself to give the best performance of an improvised one-person play *ever*. That is, until I overheard my classmates Penelope and Artie talking.

"Like, I think Clyde is a great guy and he'd probably be a great treasurer, but he's not bringing the best pop group of our time to the school!" Artie said excitedly.

"I know! I am so stoked to see Boyz Will Be Boyz," Penelope said. "They're my all-time favorite band!"

"I can't believe Chandler's cousin's best friend's boyfriend's uncle is their manager."

"I know, right? I can't believe he's getting them to come here to play a concert!"

"He definitely has my vote."

"Mine, too!" Penelope exclaimed.

" 'Ooh, Girl' is my favorite song," Artie said.

"*Ooh, girl, if I could, ooh, girl, give you the, ooh, girl . . . ,*" they sang as they walked away.

"Dang it," I said aloud. I removed my huge hat and shook my head in frustration.

"Lincoln! I've been looking all over for you. How's your stomach?"

It was Clyde. I'd been pretty much hiding from him since lunch.

"Clyde! Hi! It's, uh, feeling . . ." I paused. I couldn't keep lying to Clyde. It was time to fess up. "I've gotta tell you something, buddy. My stomach was fine. I just had some campaign plans to take care of, and I didn't think you'd love them."

"Ah. You mean the marching band thing?"

"You heard about that?"

Clyde looked down at his shoes. I could tell he was upset. "Yeah, I heard."

"I'm sorry. I just wanted to show people that you're a candidate worth celebrating!"

"What's all this? Are you going to a Renaissance festival?" he asked, pointing at my fluffy shirt.

"Oh, no. I was—okay, this is silly—After I realized the parade idea wasn't great, I came up with another idea. I was going to put on a play to get people to vote for you. But then . . ." I stopped again.

"But then what?"

"I overheard Penelope and Artie talking."

"Oh no, what'd they say? Did they say my BO was so overwhelming that they were transferring to another school instead of voting for me? Did they say my striped shirt makes me look like a bumblebee? Did they say I've had toilet paper stuck to my shoe for three hours?"

He lifted up his shoe to double-check. There wasn't any toilet paper.

"No," I sighed. "Worse."

"Did they say Chandler's cousin's best friend's boyfriend's uncle is the manager of Boyz Will Be Boyz, and he's getting them to come play a concert at the school if he wins the election that will inevitably get him all the votes for school treasurer?"

"Exactly."

Clyde sighed heavily. "It's been a good run, Lincoln, but I think I should drop out of the election."

"It's been one day."

"There's no way I can compete with a concert!"

I thought about it for a moment.

Who knows competition better than anyone?

Who could help us?

"I've got it," I said, snapping my fingers.

"Got what?" Clyde asked.

"I know who can help us find your competitive edge. Come on. Let's go to my house."

On the walk to my house, I tried to keep Clyde's spirits up by suggesting ideas that could make his campaign special. There had to be something we could do that was bigger and better than Boyz Will Be Boyz.

"What if we got a hot-air balloon and dropped snickerdoodle cookies over the school that had *Vote for Clyde* written on them in frosting?" I suggested.

"Frosting doesn't really pair well with snickerdoodles," Clyde replied.

"How about we get an airplane and hire a skywriter to write fun facts about you so other kids can get to know you?"

"Where would we get an airplane?"

"Okay, okay . . . so we set up a bounce house outside the cafeteria—"

"Lincoln, we don't have any money. We can't rent a bounce house."

"Ah. You're right. We could give away free homework help?"

"To everyone in school? We'd never get around to *our* homework."

"What if we set up a petting zoo?"

"With what animals?"

We both stopped walking.

"Lincoln, I think I should throw in the towel," Clyde said sadly.

"But what about Dr. Lopez? Pushing your boundaries? Making real changes?"

"I know, but—"

"What about getting new volleyball nets for the gym? Getting more books in the library?"

"I *know*, but—"

"What about life, liberty, and the pursuit of happiness?"

"Lincoln?"

"Sorry, that social studies lesson about the Declaration of Independence got stuck in my head."

"Understandable. I just don't know what I can do."

"Don't worry," I assured him as we started

to walk again. "My sister will know exactly what to do."

Lola was seated at the table in her room. She adjusted her tiara, poured a cup of tea, and took a sip. She raised an eyebrow and put the cup down.

"So you're worried about a little competition, hmm?" she asked. Clyde and I gulped. She may only be six, but she can be a little intimidating.

"Well, we weren't. But now we are," I said. "Clyde is running for school treasurer and everything was fine this morning, but then we found out he's running against Chandler. And Chandler is saying he's going to bring Boyz Will Be Boyz to the school. Then he gave away lollipops—"

"And plungers," Clyde added.

"Right! And plungers," I said.

"I know," Lola responded, pointing to the gigantic pile of plungers across the room on Lana's bed. "Lana asked for the leftovers from one of Chandler's friends. Don't worry, Clyde. She's still going to vote for you."

"Lola, we need a plan. We've tried everything. Please? I'll do your chores for a week," I pleaded.

"Make it two weeks, and you've got a deal."

"Done. Now what can we do?"

"Clyde, you might not like this, but it's the only way to win," she said.

Clyde looked scared. I probably did, too.

"This is just like the time I took down that monster Lindsay Sweetwater in the Little

Miss Southeastern Michigan pageant," Lola continued. "Both of us were doing a ribbon dance for the talent portion, both of us had pink sequin gowns on, and only one of us could win. Lindsay had just booked a toy commercial, and that was all anyone could talk about."

"Oh yeah! She's the girl from the Oopsie-Doodle Pootin' Poodle commercials!" Clyde exclaimed.

Lola shot him a look like she was firing lasers from her eyes.

"Anyway," she said, grimacing, "I didn't have a commercial for people to talk about, and I didn't have time to do something better than a commercial. So instead of trying to do something that made me look better than Lindsay, I did something that made her look worse than me."

"How'd you do that?" I asked. *Maybe this wasn't the best idea,* I thought. *This doesn't sound like a very Clyde thing to do.*

"I might have *slightly* exaggerated some of her 'less good' qualities," Lola said. "Maybe I even whispered those exaggerated 'less good' qualities to a few people. Maybe those people whispered to other people. Maybe all of that whispering got around to the judges. Maybe the judges believed those whispers." Lola shrugged. "Who's to say?"

"Are you saying we should make up bad stuff about Chandler and spread it around school?" Clyde asked.

"I would *never* tell you to lie, Clyde!" Lola said, clutching her necklace in shock. "I only suggest you make the bad things about Chandler sound a teensy bit worse."

"I don't know about this," Clyde said. "It doesn't seem like playing fair."

"Do you think it's fair to dangle a concert over people's heads to trick them into voting for you?" Lola asked.

"No, but that doesn't mean I should fight dirty," Clyde replied.

"I know this is tough, buddy, but Lola's won dozens and dozens of pageants. And Chandler's already fighting dirty," I said.

"The only way to beat dirty fighting is to fight dirtier," Lola said, nodding.

"I guess you're right," Clyde said. "But what would we even say?"

We borrowed Lisa's whiteboard to brainstorm ideas of what we could say about Chandler. Lola used a marker to draw a stick figure with a silly-looking face on the board and turned toward Clyde and me.

"The key to bringing someone down is pinpointing their weaknesses by using their most embarrassing moments against them. For example, if we were doing this to Lincoln, we'd bring up the fact that he still sleeps with his stuffed bunny every night," she said, emphasizing her *mean* (but true, I *guess*) point by replacing the marker cap with a loud *click*.

"You leave Bun-Bun out of this!" I said.

"Would you want everyone at school to know about Bun-Bun?" Lola asked.

"No, but that's not the point," I whimpered, folding my arms across my chest.

"Okay, whatever. Let's get down to business: What can we say about this goon?" Lola asked.

"First, I think we should avoid name-calling," Clyde said.

"Agreed," I said. "We don't want to be total jerks."

"Fiiiiiiiine," Lola said, rolling her eyes.

"What can we say about this . . . Chandler?"

"I heard he has a separate closet just for his shoes," Clyde said.

"That doesn't help us. We need something that makes him look bad," Lola said.

"How about the time he kept pushing us to give him stuff so we could get invited to his birthday party?" I suggested.

"You mean when he kept calling you Larry, and we totally took advantage of Lori?" Clyde asked. I could see Clyde's point. That time, *I* was kind of the bad guy.

"Think harder, you two!" Lola barked.

"Well, his dad works at the sewage treatment plant," Clyde said. "I bet that smell isn't easy to shake off."

"Yes! There's an idea," Lola said as she wrote *he smells* on the whiteboard.

"That's not totally true," Clyde said.

"But it could be," Lola said, shrugging.

"He once got kind of scared at a haunted house," I said.

"He got so scared he peed his pants at a haunted house built for babies," Lola said as she wrote on the whiteboard. Clyde and I looked at each other, worried. We didn't want to totally ruin his reputation, but we *did* want Clyde to win the election. Chandler had a history of being selfish, and he was not exactly the nicest guy, so he'd probably make a horrible treasurer.

"He got picked last for kickball that one time," Clyde remembered.

"Clyde, he was wearing a cast on his whole leg—he couldn't have played, anyway," I said.

"Doesn't matter! Got picked last," Lola said,

writing it down. "This is a great start."

"What happens next?" I asked.

"Yeah, do we have to tell kids these totally-not-lies-but-also-kind-of-lies about Chandler?" Clyde asked. "Won't it just come straight back to us? And won't I get disqualified? I'll have detention until I'm a hundred years old!"

"Leave the dirty work to me," Lola said, rubbing her hands together menacingly. "I don't trust you amateurs."

"Wait, did you just write *tooted in class*? We didn't say that," I said, squinting at the whiteboard where Lola was scribbling additional notes.

"It's called improvising, Linky. Now shoo! I have work to do."

Clyde and I decided it was probably better to stop asking questions. I mean, if anyone can make someone else look bad, it's Lola. She once threatened to tell on me and my other sisters to our parents if we didn't do all sorts of ridiculous favors for her. She made our sporty older sister Lynn give her a pedicure. Lynn didn't even cut her own toenails, and I don't think she'd ever opened a bottle of nail polish before. Lola gets whatever she wants, however she needs to go about getting it. She'd be able to turn Clyde's campaign around in no time.

As I walked him to the front door, Clyde still looked nervous. He's probably the second-nicest person I know (the first being my older sister Leni, who just might be the nicest human being on the planet), and he hates to do things that seem like they might be against the rules or could hurt someone's feelings. But it was like Lola said: the only way to beat dirty fighting was to fight dirtier. Right?

"I hope we're doing the right thing," Clyde said as he turned the knob.

"Don't worry, buddy. It'll all be worth it when you're treasurer and you can help those in need. Remember the volleyball nets."

"I'll remember the volleyball nets. See you tomorrow at school," Clyde said, sighing.

I hope this works.

The next day at school, Lola's plan was already in effect. Kids were whispering in the halls to each other before the first bell had even rung. I was putting my books away in my locker when I heard Joy talking to Penelope nearby.

"I heard he was so scared, he not only wet his pants but started *crying*," Joy told Penelope.

"Well, I heard he was so scared, he accidentally called the kid with him *Mommy*," Penelope said to Joy.

"He was so scared that not only did he do all those things, but he also refused to go to sleep for a month without having his dad check his closet for monsters *and* turn on a night-light!" Artie chimed in as he walked by.

"Wooooooow," Joy and Penelope said incredulously.

It was amazing what a story could turn into if enough people passed it around. Definitely a dangerous tool in the wrong hands, and probably not the nicest thing you could do to a person, but this was for a good cause. Clyde is a good guy. He just needed a boost, that's all. It was like saying the roll didn't count if the dice fell off the table during a board game. It was harmless, but it could change the outcome of the game.

"Well, I don't know if I want to vote for someone who gets scared that easily, no matter how much I love Boyz Will Be Boyz. It was just a bunny rabbit, after all," Joy said to Penelope and Artie.

"I mean, I'm president of the Royal Woods chapter of the B-Dub-Double-B official fan club, and *I'm* considering voting for Clyde, even if that means missing a concert," Artie said.

Joy and Penelope nodded in agreement as the three of them walked down the hall. *Take that, Chandler! Three more votes for Clyde!* I couldn't wait to tell Clyde the good news. I finished up at my locker and walked to class.

When I got to the classroom, Liam, Zach, Rusty, and Stella were already talking to Clyde.

His expression was changing quickly based on whatever the squad was telling him. One moment he looked like he got the best birthday present ever, then like he just ate an old tuna sandwich, then like he just saw a ghost-robot-monster attacking his Nana Gayle. I walked over and joined them.

"I heard he stinks to the high rafters, worse than goat manure!" Liam said as I approached.

"I heard he's been picked last for every sport in gym for the last four years," Rusty said.

"I heard he's so gassy, he goes to a special government-funded science lab after school every day just to keep himself from exploding!" Zach said.

"I heard he doesn't even have a connection to Boyz Will Be Boyz and it's all a big lie," Stella said.

Clyde turned green. "Lincoln, a word?" he asked as he scooted me away from our friends.

"What's up, buddy?" I asked quietly.

"This is too much," Clyde whispered. "I can't handle the pressure of hearing all these lies. I know he's not exactly the best person, but—"

"I overheard three more people saying they're going to vote for you!" I interjected.

"Wow, really?"

"Yeah, they were definitely going to vote for Chandler, and now they're not. I know this isn't the way you want to do it, but you've gotta trust me as your campaign manager. Have I ever steered you wrong before?"

"I mean, there was that one time with the cotton candy, and that time with the pony ride, and that other time. . . ." Clyde's words trailed off. "Sorry, Lincoln. I trust you. I know this will all work out. I'm going to talk to the kids in the after-school program later to find out how I can help them if I become treasurer. I heard they still haven't gotten a single new crayon for any of the classes this year. Kids are coloring with broken, unlabeled stubs of wax!"

"You do that, Clyde. I've got to keep up this momentum. As your campaign manager, I advise we turn up the heat and secure this election."

Clyde nodded and we high-fived. I couldn't stop thinking about how I could help Clyde win. Lola's plan had worked so well. There had to be something else that effective.

After school, Clyde and I went our separate ways. On my walk home, I kept thinking about

Lola's successful plan. I stopped suddenly. *Wait a minute!* All *of my sisters are really talented and smart. If one of my sisters had a great idea that helped Clyde, imagine what would happen if I asked all ten!*

I called a sibling meeting. I asked everyone to join me in Lori and Leni's room, even Lily, the baby. I took my shoe and knocked it on Leni's sewing table like a gavel.

Thunk thunk thunk!

"I call this meeting to order!" I shouted.

"Shall we go over the minutes from our

last meeting?" Lisa asked as she unrolled a never-ending scroll of notes.

"That sounds like a *tearable* idea," Luan said. "Get it?"

We all groaned.

"I literally have a million things I could be doing," Lori said. "What do you want, Lincoln?"

"You know how Clyde is running for treasurer? And I'm his campaign manager?" I asked. "And how this is really important to us? And how Clyde is practically family? And how great a treasurer he'd be?"

"We know, dude. You've been talking about it nonstop all week," Luna said, plucking at her guitar strings. My other sisters all nodded and rolled their eyes in agreement.

"Anyway, Lola helped us out with a strategy,

and it was really amazing—"

"Thank you, thank you," Lola said, curtsying.

"But it wasn't quite enough," I said as Lola shot me an angry look. "Chandler's still in the lead, and I'm out of ideas. Listen, I know you're all really great at totally different things and you all have different talents, so . . . can you help us? You may be the only hope Clyde has of beating Chandler." I paused. My sisters were looking around the room at each other, trying to decide what to do. "Please?"

"Of course we'll help you, bro," Lynn said as she playfully socked me on the shoulder.

"That's what family's for," Lana said. "Oooh! Oooh! I'll bet El Diablo can help us!" She was referring to her very large snake.

"Um, maybe El Diablo should stay home,"

I replied. "But I like that you're thinking outside the box!"

All ten of my sisters started talking at the same time.

"I can write an unforgettable jingle!" Luna shouted, strumming a chord on her guitar.

"I can use my robot Todd to poll our classmates and create a spreadsheet of voter statistics," Lisa added.

"I'll literally make Clyde the most popular kid at your school overnight," said Lori.

"I'll make anyone thinking of voting for Chandler think twice," Lynn said as she flexed her biceps.

"I already did my part," Lola noted with a shrug.

"Hops and I are on the case!" Lana cried, high-fiving the tongue of her pet frog. *At least it's not her snake.*

"I *treasure* the opportunity to help your best friend!" Luan said as we all groaned again.

"I'll bring out the ruffled blouses, costume jewelry, and eye patches!" Leni said, carrying an armful of fake jewelry. We all looked at her, confused. "For the *treasure.* Gosh."

Lily murmured in baby talk and handed me her teddy bear.

"Thanks, Lil," I said, holding the bear.

"And I can read Clyde's cards," our spooky sister Lucy said.

"AHHHHH!" we screamed. Lucy had a habit of popping up out of nowhere and accidentally scaring the rest of us.

Sometimes it's hard having a big family, but it's great knowing they always have my back. My sisters didn't even hesitate; they already knew how to use their skills to help. The eleven of us hung out in Lori and Leni's room until dinner, plotting and planning. Together, we could help Clyde win. Operation All the Louds Group Together to Use Their Different Ideas to Help Clyde Win and Also Come Up with a Shorter Name for This Plan was a go!

The next morning, I woke up before my alarm. I couldn't wait to get to school. Today was the day we put my sisters' plans into action, and there was no time to waste! I was first downstairs and made lunches for all my sisters and myself so we'd be able to get out the door the second everyone finished their morning routines.

Lisa, Lola, Lana, and Lucy all go to school with Clyde and me, so it was easier for them to help us. My other sisters had to be a bit more creative with how they helped, since they go to the middle school and the high school.

Lori's goal was to make Clyde the most popular kid at our school. She was stopping every kid at her high school who had a younger sibling at our school just so she could tell them to tell their little brother or sister to vote for Clyde. Artie, who had a big brother at the high school, heard about it almost immediately. And it didn't take long for Lori's pleas to get on her classmates' nerves.

"My brother told me she was the obvious choice for Spring Blossom Dance Duchess, but he said that since she's putting all this energy into Clyde, she's now losing to Carol Pingrey,"

Artie told me. Carol Pingrey is my sister's nemesis. She and Lori have been competing since they were in kindergarten. *I hope Lori isn't too mad about this.*

"Oh no, that stinks!" I replied. "But . . . do you think more people here are planning to vote for Clyde?"

Artie scoffed. "I doubt it. I haven't done what my big brother's told me to do since I was in diapers," he said, patting my shoulder as he walked away. *Gulp. Okay, Lincoln. That's just one plan. Everything will be fine,* I thought as I tried not to worry.

"*Ahhhhhhhhhhhhhhhhhhhhhhh!*" screamed a group of terrified kids as they ran out of a classroom followed by a near-zoo number of reptiles and amphibians, each with *Vote for Clyde* painted on their backs. Snakes, toads, iguanas, turtles—you name it. *Dang it. This must be Lana's doing!* I rubbed the top of my nose with my thumb and pointer finger as I watched my sister chase after her slimy and scaly creatures.

"Lana!" I called. "You said you and *Hops* were on it. One frog, not a whole pond full! And I told you no snakes!"

"No way," she shouted as she continued down the hall after her pets. "You just said no El Diablo! I left him at home!"

Double dang it.

As I walked down the hall, I noticed Chandler had added small posters to the wall. At first I just thought it was the paint chipping— some parts of the school could use a little bit of help—but they were pieces of paper. I stopped to read one.

" 'Chandler Presents Boyz Will Be Boyz: A Winner's Concert. On the blacktop after school. After I win. Vote for me,' " I read aloud. On the posters, under the words, there was a picture of Chandler posing with all four members of the music group. I couldn't tell if the photo was real or fake, but it didn't matter. It was convincing. Lizards and persuasive big brothers wouldn't be enough to win this election. We needed more.

At lunch, as I was going to meet my friends at our favorite outdoor picnic table, I heard the familiar sound of a guitar amp turning on. I rounded a corner and was surprised to see Luna and her British roadie, Chunk. They had just set up her gear, and it looked like she was getting ready to jam.

"Hey, little bro," she called to me.

"Luna, what are you doing here?" I asked.

"I'm here to rock the vote! I've been teaching Principal Huggins how to play the ukulele, so he let me come hold an impromptu concert for the Clydesdale!"

"A concert?"

"Well, not a whole light-show-and-fireworks-and-encore kinda concert, but he said I could play a quick little tune during your lunch period."

A crowd gathered around Luna as she tuned her guitar. The amp crackled a bit, and some feedback screeched out of the speaker. The crowd jumped, startled by the high-pitched noise.

"Hey, Lincoln!"

"Hey, Clyde! I was looking for you!"

"I had a dentist appointment this morning, so my dads just dropped me off at school," Clyde said, smiling. His teeth were so clean, I could swear they were sparkling.

"Oh yeah! They look great!"

"Um, Lincoln?"

"Yeah, Clyde?"

"What's Luna doing here?" He gestured to my sister.

Crud. I forgot to tell Clyde! How'd I forget to tell Clyde?

"So, you know how Lola's plan helped us get more votes?"

Clyde sighed. "Lincoln, you know how I feel about all that negativity. My Nana Gayle would be so disappointed in me for stooping so low."

"I know, I know. But it helped, right?"

"Yeah," Clyde said, a little bummed out. "It helped, I guess."

"So I had a great idea on the way home. Ten sisters means ten great ideas that can help us!"

"I know I got a B-plus on that last test, but I think your math might be off on this one."

"Just think of it, Clyde!" I said, putting my arm around his shoulder. "They're all really good at different stuff. And that stuff is different than what we're good at, right?"

"Yeah, but—"

"So they can probably get to kids we wouldn't be able to get to! They'll help us reach a broader audience!"

"I guess, but—"

"And a broader audience means more votes! More votes means beating Chandler! You'll go down in history as the kid who beat the other kid who was trying to bribe kids with plungers and boy bands!"

"I'm not so sure about this, Lincoln. What happened to being the most *me* I can be? Like what my dad told us got him votes when he ran for vice president in college? What happened to volleyball nets?"

"You can do all that stuff *after* you win," I assured him. Besides, once my sisters decide they're going to do something, there's really no stopping them. If they were a weather pattern, they'd be an unstoppable sisternado. "Now let's give Luna's song a listen. I'm sure it will be great. Everyone will love it."

We sat down by Luna. Her guitar was all tuned up and she was ready to rock. She began strumming the strings. It was a really catchy melody. Then she started singing along.

"*Clyde McBride. Clyde McBride.*

He's super great; he's never lied!

For student council, he's qualified.

Your future treasurer, Clyde McBride!"

I had to hand it to my sister. The song was awesome! She had the other kids singing along in no time. The crowd was cheering. Everyone was chanting Clyde's name! Maybe the plan would work out. Maybe ten sisters *were* enough to beat the chart-topping, award-winning, stadium-sell-out Boyz Will Be Boyz. Oh, and Chandler.

We had PE after lunch. And when PE was over, I could hear kids humming Luna's song in the hall. I smiled as I walked toward Mrs. Johnson's classroom, happy Luna's help seemed to have paid off. Everything was going great! That is, until I got into the classroom and saw a group of kids all wearing matching tie-dyed

CHANDLER FOR TREASURER shirts. I guess Clyde hadn't noticed. He was busy talking to Girl Jordan and Joy over by his desk.

"So you're saying your after-school painting class only has three tubes of paint?" Clyde asked Girl Jordan in disbelief.

"Yeah," Girl Jordan said, sounding disappointed. "Right when Miss Patterson was about to show us how to paint mermaids and sea stars, she realized there wasn't enough paint to go around, so we shared canvases. It used to be my favorite after-school activity, but now I don't even know if I want to go anymore."

"Aw man, that sounds awful! And, Joy, you said you've lost *five dollars* in the vending machine this year?"

"Yeah! Sometimes you want a snack for the walk home from school, right?" Joy said. Clyde and Girl Jordan nodded in agreement. "And I keep trying, like maybe the school has fixed the machine, but that's a big honkin' no."

Clyde shook his head. "I'm sorry. I can't believe the machine ate five dollars. That's a whole meal at Burpin' Burger!"

"Or a tube of paint," Girl Jordan added.

"Thanks for listening, Clyde," Joy said. "Good luck with the election!"

Joy and Girl Jordan left to go sit down at their desks.

"Hey, Lincoln," Clyde said as I sat down at the desk next to his. He sounded a little defeated.

"What's up, buddy?" I asked. *It must be the Chandler shirts.*

"I'm feeling a little scared. The more I talk to people, the more it sounds like a lot of stuff needs to be fixed around the school. I don't know if I'm the kid to do it."

"Of course you are. Just keep your head up. You've got this!"

"Thanks. Hey, Lincoln?"

"Yeah, Clyde?"

"Do you think one of your sisters has something up her sleeve better than tie-dyed shirts?"

"I sure hope so," I said, trying not to sound worried. So far only Lola's and Luna's plans had had any effect, but they still weren't quite T-shirt or pop-band level. I had my fingers crossed.

We were reading about the invention of the printing press when I saw Lisa and her robot

Todd in the hallway waving to me. I got a hall pass from Mrs. Johnson and met them outside my classroom.

"Lisa, shouldn't you be in class?" Even though Lisa was a genius, she was in kindergarten at my school—but only because my parents thought she was too young to go to college. She rolled her eyes at me.

"Ms. Shrinivas knows where I am. Older sibling, I've been using Todd's beta polling software to form a strategy for your friend Clyde," she said as she briefly removed her glasses to wipe them on her shirt. I looked at her blankly.

"What does that mean?"

"Frankly, it doesn't look good. Todd polled all of the kindergarten, first-, second-, and third-grade classes already. Chandler is way ahead for all four grades. It seems none of those kids were present for Luna's serenade at lunch, and they seem to value music and lollipops over hard facts."

"What about the fourth and fifth graders?"

"Those could go either way."

We heard a loud crash down the hall followed by the *brrrttt brrrttt* of what sounded like a dozen whoopee cushions and the cackling laugh of our sister.

"Luan!" Lisa and I cried as we dashed toward the noise.

Luan was in the library juggling books and telling jokes, perched on her unicycle, when we got there. The librarian looked like she was about to pull her hair out from stress.

"Why was the skunk arrested for counterfeiting? 'Cause he gave out bad *cents*.

Get it? *Ha ha ha ha ha!*" Luan chuckled as the crowd groaned. "Why's money called *dough*? Because we all *knead* it! *Ha ha ha ha ha!*" The crowd groaned again.

"Luan, what are you doing here?" I asked.

"Oh, hey, Lincoln! Hey, Lisa! I didn't have to go to study hall today, so I figured I'd stop by. Trying to make these folks laugh, but I seem to be getting a bad *read* on them. *Dewey* think their senses of humor need to be *renewed*? I'm worried they may throw the *book* at me. *Ha ha ha ha ha!*" Lisa and I sighed. We were used to Luan's over-the-top sense of humor.

"Well, I'm not sure this is working," I said, trying to coax her out of the library. "So how about we *roll* out of here?" I gestured to her unicycle.

"I'm getting new output from Todd," Lisa

said, typing something into the body of her robot. "*Tsk, tsk.* He's testing the body heat and brain wave functionality in this room. Based on the data, it looks like Luan's comedy routine had the opposite effect than we'd hoped."

"Come on, Luan," I said. "Let's go before Clyde loses any more votes."

"You've been a lovely audience. I'll be performing next month at Sadie's bat mitzvah! Hope to see you all there!" Luan waved to the relieved audience, and we escorted her out the door.

We'd barely made it three feet from the library, when we came across my spooky younger sister, Lucy. She was sitting at a table with her crystal ball, talking to a kid from her class. It was like I couldn't turn a corner without running into one of my sisters!

"Hmm . . . your future doesn't look so bright," Lucy said, shaking her head. "If you do not clean your room, you will find certain doom. To avoid this murky tide, change your fate with a vote for Clyde."

"Aaaahhhh!" the kid screamed, and he ran away from Lucy as fast as his legs could take him.

"Lucy!" I exclaimed. "You said you'd read *Clyde's* cards, not do—well . . . whatever *this* is!"

"I did read his cards, but then the spirit of Great-Grandma Harriet encouraged me to reach out to the mortal world on his behalf," Lucy said.

"Can you try to be a little less . . . well . . ." Lucy's bat, Fangs, flew over out of nowhere and landed on her shoulder. Lisa, Luan, and I jumped. "Spooky?"

"Sigh. I never get to have any fun."

"Sorry, Luce. Maybe you and Great-Grandma Harriet can find another way to help Clyde," I said. "I have to get back to class. Try to keep the chaos to a minimum, everyone!"

"Where'd you go?" Clyde asked me when I got back to my desk.

"It's a long story," I said. "My sisters are trying really hard to get you elected, that's for sure."

"It's so nice of them to help out," Clyde said, beaming. "You know, I talk to Dr. Lopez sometimes about how lonely it can be as an only child, but she reminds me that your family is kind of like a second family to me, and that really helps."

I couldn't tell Clyde about Luan's bad jokes or Lucy's crystal ball reading. Maybe Lynn's and Leni's plans would work better.

"Dang it, Lincoln!" Liam shouted. "I can't git yer sister's song outta my ding-dang ear holes!"

Oh no.

"Ugh, same here," said Stella, removing earmuffs from her head. "I tried using these to block out all the sound, and then I realized it was stuck in my head."

Uh-oh.

"Me too!" Rusty added. "But don't worry, guys. I downloaded the newest Boyz Will Be

Boyz album to help us forget."

I shot Rusty a look. *Come on, man. Anything but Boyz Will Be Boyz.*

"Luna's song is just catchy, that's all! It's a catchy tune!" I said.

"Um, Lincoln? Maybe Luna's song wasn't as great as we thought it was," Clyde said. He looked worried.

"I know, but maybe—"

"And when you left earlier, Chandler was handing out passes to tour the sewage plant."

"Don't worry, Clyde! We've still got Lynn and Leni!"

The sound of a locker crashing closed startled our whole class and drove us into the hall to see what was causing the ruckus.

"YOU STAY IN THERE UNTIL YOU KNOW WHO YOU'RE VOTING FOR!

Oh hey, Stinkin'!"

Dang it.

"Lynn, what are you doing?"

"It's what we talked about. You know, helping Clyde! What up, Clydesdale?" Lynn hollered down the hall, in front of my whole class.

"Uh, Lynn, I don't think this is the best idea," I said, trying to gesture to the rest of my classmates so she'd get the hint.

"Nah, he'll be fine. Why are you pointing at those nerds? Do you think one of them needs to be reminded to vote for Clyde, too?" she asked, holding her knuckles menacingly. My whole class gasped and took a step back. Even Mrs. Johnson.

Gulp. "No, we're all good, Lynn," I said, inching away from my sister. I faced my classmates and Mrs. Johnson. "Nothing to see here, folks. Just a faulty locker. Let's go back to learning about the order of operations."

"Lincoln, we were discussing atoms and molecules," Mrs. Johnson said.

"That's what I meant! Let's get cracking on some molecules!" I was sweating all over. I knew they meant well and they weren't trying to sabotage us, but I was starting to think my sisters' skills were not exactly campaign-ready. Just as we were all walking into our classroom, one of Chandler's friends ran down the hall with a megaphone.

"REMINDER TO ALL STUDENTS!" the kid shouted through the megaphone. "WHEN CHANDLER WINS, WE GET A FREE CONCERT! VOTE FOR CHANDLER! ONE KID WILL GET A CHANCE TO MEET

BOYZ WILL BE BOYZ! THAT COULD BE YOU!"

"Oooh, I love Boyz Will Be Boyz!" Mrs. Johnson said enthusiastically.

Next to me, my classmates cheered and Clyde fainted. I nearly fainted, too. I sat Clyde up and did my best to reassure him that we were still in a good spot. It was getting harder to convince him (and myself) that everything was going to be okay and we were still in this race.

"Don't worry, Clyde. We still have— LENI?!"

My second-oldest sister, Leni, was wearing an eyepatch and a pirate costume with our family bird, Walt, perched on her shoulder and was dragging a large wooden chest behind her.

"Oh, hey, Lincoln! I think I got a little

confused. Is Clyde the treasure or does he bury the treasure?" she asked, holding a fist full of plastic sparkling jewelry in one hand.

Clyde was moving to get up, until he caught a glimpse of pirate Leni and quickly went back down again.

"Treasur*er*, Leni. Not *treasure*," I said as she looked at me blankly. "Why don't you try burying that treasure in the backyard?"

"Okay!" She smiled and went back to dragging the chest down the hall.

With no other distractions, our class returned to the classroom. I helped Clyde stand up. He really looked defeated.

"Everything is going great, Clyde! Nothing to worry about!" I said through gritted teeth.

"Campaign meeting. Your house. After school," Clyde said.

Clyde and I walked in silence to my house after school. He was fuming. I could almost see smoke coming out of his ears. I didn't know what to say. My sisters and I were only trying to help Clyde win. He couldn't be *that* mad at me, could he?

When we got to my house, we went straight

upstairs to my room. We didn't even make our usual kitchen pit stop to get snacks. We were nearly at my bedroom door when Lisa popped out of her and Lily's room, next to mine, with her robot Todd.

"Ah, Lincoln! Just the person I was looking for. Listen, Todd's got the poll results from today's campaign efforts—"

"Not now, Lisa," I said, looking at Clyde, who's jaw was so tightly clenched that it looked like he was about to grind his teeth into dust.

"But, older sibling, I really must inform you that the numbers are—"

"Not now, Lisa," I said again, gesturing to Clyde, whose left eye was starting to twitch. Lisa ignored my cue.

"The numbers are catastrophically dismal. Or, in layman's terms: Clyde has no chance of winning," Lisa said as she shuffled some papers in her hands.

"THAT'S IT!" Clyde screamed. Lisa and I yelped.

"Toodle-oo!" Lisa said as she retreated back to her room.

"LET'S GO!" Clyde yelled as he pulled me into my room and shut the door.

"Clyde, listen—"

"No, Lincoln. It's *your* turn to listen. I'm sorry I yelled at you, but I am really, really, really mad."

"Why are you mad? I know the results aren't great, but we were only trying to help," I said as I looked down at my shoes.

"Who were you helping, Lincoln? None of this was ever the plan! You took me out of my own election! I just wanted to prove that

I could do this! How could you stand there and keep telling me it was going to be okay?" Clyde folded his arms and looked away.

"I was trying to . . ." I paused. What was I doing? Clyde was right. I *hadn't* been keeping him in mind. I had only been thinking about how I could appear to be the best campaign manager. I hadn't talked to my sisters about what they were going to do to make sure they had Clyde in mind. I'd given everyone free rein to be themselves *except* Clyde.

Clyde had never been this mad at me before, not even the time I accidentally broke his limited-edition One-Eyed Jack watch last year or even the time I accidentally blamed him for the disappearance of the class hamster in second grade. We never fight. Clyde is the kind of person who is good at accepting apologies.

He lets his friends make mistakes. Suddenly, I felt terrible.

"Clyde, I'm so sorry. I messed up. Like, really, really bad. I had no idea how completely out of control everything had become," I said. "Please let me make it up to you. We can do everything your way. I won't get anyone else involved. I promise."

I meant it, every word. I had let down my very best friend in the whole world. There was no grosser feeling than that—not even the feeling in your stomach after you ate expired pudding at Aunt Ruth's house.

For what felt like forever and a day, Clyde didn't say anything. *Will I have to find a new best friend? Where does one even find someone like Clyde? He's one of a kind!*

"Apology accepted," Clyde said.

"Are we still friends?" I asked.

"*Best* friends," Clyde reassured me. We hugged and did our awesome best-friend handshake.

"Thanks, buddy," I said. "Now, what are we going to do about your campaign?"

"Honestly, I think I should drop out. Chandler's going to win."

"No way! Listen, I know I told you we can do everything your way, but I can't let you drop out of this race."

"But there's no way I can get ahead now! Chandler's been giving stuff away left and right. You and your sisters," he said, "were a little intense."

"Okay, but we still have the candidate presentations before the vote on Thursday!"

"Lincoln, there's no *way* I'll have a better

presentation than Chandler. He'll probably have the real Santa Claus onstage, for all we know!"

"Clyde, you can do this. Remember how your dad said he won? He said he was honest and he was himself."

"So?"

"So we haven't tried that in your campaign yet. Why don't you go out there and just be Clyde?"

"You really think that will work?"

"I know it will. Now let's do this!"

Clyde and I worked hard preparing for his presentation. I mostly just hung out for support, getting him juice boxes when his energy ran low as he feverishly wrote down ideas. Clyde didn't have any talents that could double as performances for a big crowd. Though it was impressive he could figure out the date of any antique just by looking at it, that didn't quite translate to the stage, so Clyde decided to write a speech. He was going to conquer his fear of public speaking while convincing the whole school that he'd be a better candidate.

It was a big deal.

Thursday came around quickly. Was there part of me that thought Clyde was totally doomed? Yes, yes, there was. But it was worth trying as hard as we could to win this election.

We got to the auditorium and waited backstage as the candidates for school council secretary finished giving their speeches.

"I should've run for secretary," Clyde said, looking at the super-calm kids leaving the stage. A few claps and a cough came from the audience. The lights went down.

BWOW BWOW BWOOOOOOW! Loud

music blared from the speakers.

"ARE YOU READY, KIDS?!" a voice boomed.

The crowd roared.

"I CAN'T HEAR YOU!"

They screamed even louder. Clyde and I had to cover our ears.

"THE SUPERCOOL KID YOU ALL KNOW AND LOVE: CHANDLER 'ENTER CHANDMAN' McCANN!"

The whole stage lit up and Chandler appeared. The crowd oohed and aahed. He had on a headset microphone like one of those people on the shopping channel. Two of his friends were onstage, throwing candy to the audience. It felt as if everyone was cheering louder than they'd ever cheered in their lives.

"Whaddup, Royal Woods Elementary! I'm

the Chandman, and I'm here to be your school council guy!"

"I don't think he knows what he's running for," I whispered to Clyde as my younger sisters joined us in the wings of the stage.

"As your treasure dude, I will totally get my best buds Boyz Will Be Boyz to come play just for you!"

"I heard he actually does know them," Clyde whispered to me. "One of the Boyz is Chandler's second cousin's best friend's brother's bunkmate from summer camp."

"I heard it was his babysitter's sister's teacher's cousin," Lucy said.

"Huh, I heard it was his dad's childhood friend's niece's piano teacher," Lana said.

"It doesn't matter if he knows them or not. Knowing them won't make him a good treasurer," I said, rolling my eyes.

"If I win, the school will be awesome!" Chandler continued. "And I will tell you right now"—he dropped his voice low, frowned, and spoke quietly into the microphone—"if you don't vote for me, you will be banned for *life* from my annual birthday bash." The smile returned to Chandler's face, and his voice perked up. "Vote for the Chandman! GOOD NIGHT, ROYAL WOODS ELEMENTARY!"

A confetti canon shot glitter, and balloons came out from a trapdoor in the stage. It was bananas! The crowd was going wild!

Clyde didn't have an icicle's chance on the sun.

It was like a ghost appeared in front of the crowd when Clyde walked onstage. One of the teachers adjusted a microphone on a stand to Clyde's height. The feedback from the mic *squeeeeaked,* and the kids in the audience all responded with winces and boos. The stage floor creaked under Clyde's feet. Somebody in the audience cleared their throat. Clyde was totally toast.

"My fellow students," he said, shuffling papers in his hand.

"He's *dying* out there!" Lola whispered.

"Maybe we should go onstage and help him somehow," Lana suggested.

"No, let's give him a chance!" I said.

"Todd is picking up a lot of snoring," Lisa said as she examined the reading from her robot. "It's looking bleak."

"Come on, guys," I urged. "We've gotta at least *try* to support him! Even if he's falling flat on his face."

We focused on Clyde. He hadn't said another word. You could almost hear crickets it was so quiet. If someone had dropped a pencil, it would have sounded louder than a cymbal crash.

"Listen, I'm going to be honest with you, I am terrified right now," Clyde said, laughing a little. "It's silly, really. I've spent a lot of the last week trying to get to know those of you I didn't know, which was also really scary for me, but right now, I feel like I'm talking to strangers. I shouldn't, though, you know?"

A few people in the crowd giggled.

"I think they're laughing *with* him," Lana said.

"I think you're right," I said with a smile.

"I don't have any candy to give you," Clyde said. The crowd *awwwed.* "I wish I did. And I don't have any second cousins with connections to cool bands, though I *do* love Boyz Will Be Boyz's less-celebrated second album. But here's what I do have. I have information you've given me," he said, gesturing to the audience.

My older sisters came to join us backstage.

"What'd we miss?" Lori asked. We looked at them. "What? We got a pass to come here. This is too important."

"Yeah, little bro," Luna said, nudging me with her elbow. "We couldn't miss our *other* brother's shot at politics!"

"Will you please *shhh*!" Lola commanded, putting her finger up to her lips to shush our chattier sisters.

"I know that our volleyball nets have had holes in them ever since we had the Michigan Fencers Association tournament here. I know our librarian has a list of books she wants to get but can't afford. And they're books we want! Like Bill Buck's *Comic Writing Guide for Comic Lovers Who Love Comics* or the rest of the Princess Pony series," he said, shooting

Lucy a look. Lucy blushed. She loves ghosts and ghouls more than most people do, but she also secretly loves the Princess Pony books. Like, a lot.

"Girl Jordan told me there's no paint for the after-school art program. Joy told me the vending machine has eaten a bunch of her money. Petey Wimple told me one of the two swings on the kindergarten playground has been broken since the beginning of the school year. One swing for all those kindergartners? That's baloney!"

Some of the kids in the crowd clapped and hollered.

"You tell 'em, Clyde!" Liam shouted.

"Yeah, Clyde! What else is baloney?" Rusty added.

Clyde took the microphone off the stand

with confidence and walked to the edge of the stage.

"It's baloney that we only have one dance a year! Dances are fun! We get to listen to music and hang out in the gym after school!"

"YEAH!" a bunch of the kids cheered.

"It's baloney that we don't have more school-spirit days! What's more fun than coming to school in your pajamas?!"

More cheers.

"And it's baloney that our past treasurers haven't fixed any of these things, even though they totally could've at least tried! That is what your treasurer is supposed to do! That's the job, and I am ready for it!"

The crowd burst into applause.

"Royal Woods Elementary, I want to represent you—*all* of you. Everyone from the kindergartners to the custodial staff and back again. I want to make sure that our student council fund-raisers bring money back to the things we need and want as a school. Hey, I might not win this election. I get it." Clyde stopped for a moment and took a breath. It felt just as quiet as when he'd started talking—but this time in a good way.

"But if I'm elected, I will try to get those paints for the art club. I will try to replace those nets. I will try to get new snack vending machines or at least get the ones we have fixed. And I promise, if I'm elected, I will always be available to lend an ear and listen to your suggestions, because there's no *I* in *Royal Woods Elementary School* or in *treasurer.* Thank you for your time," Clyde said, bowing.

The whole audience stood up and started

clapping and cheering their heads off. When Clyde came backstage, my sisters and I gave him a big group hug.

"Clyde, that was amazing!" I said. "I'm so proud of you, buddy!"

"Clyde, my dude, you're totally an all-star!" Luna said.

"I could not be happier about your additions to the library," Lucy said in her monotone voice.

"Trust me, she really couldn't be happier," I said.

Luan shrugged. "Could've used a few more laughs."

"You, like, totally didn't even need our help to bury treasure," Leni added.

"What?" Clyde asked.

"Don't worry, I'll explain it to you later," I said. "Let's go get ready for the vote."

My older sisters said their goodbyes and wished Clyde good luck. The rest of us headed to the polls that our teachers had set up in the cafeteria. They tried to make them as realistic as possible, so we had to wait in line to give our votes.

Lisa stood by the exit with her robot and

had Todd track kids as they came out so she could figure out who was in the lead. Lana and Lola weaved through the line, listening to other kids talk about the speeches.

"I thought it might be a harder decision, but as the chapter president, I just can't turn my back on Boyz Will Be Boyz. 'Ooh, Girl' is my all-time favorite jam!" Lucy overheard Artie say to another kid.

"I'm voting for Clyde because I'm totally tired of playing volleyball with a busted net," Lana heard Sammie say.

"I'm undecided," a third grader said.

"Gosh, just pick one!" Lola screamed back. "And it'd better be Clyde."

Principal Huggins appeared over her and cleared his throat.

"Miss Loud, I think you should get in line

to cast your vote," he said to Lola.

"Yes, Principal Huggins," Lola said in her nicest voice while curtsying. As soon as he turned away, she gave the third grader a mean look and gestured that she'd be watching him.

Clyde and I were so nervous, we were shaking. Our friends voted and came up to talk to us.

"Your speech was amazing, Clyde," Stella said.

"Totally," Rusty added. "I mean, am I going to be sad to miss the concert of a lifetime? Probably. Was it worth it to vote for my buddy? Maybe!"

"I reckon that was the best speech in Royal Woods Elementary School history!" Liam said. "You brought down the house faster than a goat kickin' a lantern in a barn fulla hay!" We all stared at him. We had no idea what he was talking about.

"Sorry, Clyde. I didn't vote. Can't have them tracking me," Zach said as he looked around suspiciously. Stella opened her mouth to say something but stopped herself. There was no logic with Zach.

"Good luck, Clyde!" Stella said as our group waved to us and walked away.

The line was still really long. My sisters and Clyde and I had all already voted, and we were just waiting with Lisa to look at her tallies. It was totally neck and neck. Todd wasn't giving us any new data, and it was taking forever for everyone to get through the voting line.

"Loud family, Mr. McBride, I think it's time you all went home. Some of the other children have been mentioning that they are a little scared of the robot," Principal Huggins said to us. "I'm a little freaked out by that metal box myself."

"WHO. ARE. YOU. CALLING. A. BOX?" Todd asked. Principal Huggins jumped back. *"Aaaah!"* He cleared his throat and adjusted his tie. "Louds, McBride. Home. Now. We're going to tally up the votes tonight, and we'll announce the results tomorrow."

Clyde and I could barely sleep. We were both up most of the night, checking in with each other on our walkie-talkies every five minutes. Way, way past either of our bedtimes, we finally decided we should try to at least close our eyes.

In the morning, Clyde and I went to school together. We practically ran all the way. We were so excited, we didn't even *talk* until we got to our lockers, which is saying a lot for us.

"Holy moly, Lincoln! What if I get elected? What if enough people voted for me? What if I become treasurer and become a popular kid and then we're separated at lunch? What if we start drifting off as I pursue a life of politics, and then by the time we get to high school, we don't even talk anymore?"

"Clyde."

"Or what if I *don't* get elected? What if kids start booing me when I enter rooms? What if I got a bunch of kids banned for life from Chandler's birthday party and they hold me responsible and never speak to me again and start spreading rumors about me and then I have to transfer to another school?"

"Clyde."

"Or what if it was a tie and we have to do the whole election all over again? What if it was a dream? What if it was a *dog's* dream and we don't even exist?"

"CLYDE!"

"I did it again, huh?" Clyde asked between breaths into a paper bag.

"Yup." I patted his back. "Don't worry, buddy. No matter what happens, you did your Clydest. You were the Clydest Clyde you could be, and that means way more than the results of an election."

"You're right, Lincoln. It doesn't matter if I won. I tried really hard."

"You did!"

"I did things I was scared to do, like giving that speech!"

"Yeah!"

"I am awesome!"

"You sure are!"

We high-fived and went to class.

We expected to hear about the election results right away, but we didn't. The day dragged on at the slowest possible pace. It was worse than the last day of school, right before summer vacation starts. School was almost over by the time we heard the loudspeaker crackle.

"Okay, students. You've waited; we've counted," Principal Huggins said over the loudspeaker. "The results are in. . . ."

Clyde and I walked in silence back to my house. We wanted to deliver the news personally to my sisters.

When we walked through the door, my sisters were all gathered on the couch getting ready to watch their favorite show, *The Dream Boat*. They all stared at us. Luna grabbed the remote to mute the TV. Clyde and I sighed. My sisters all held their breath. For the first time probably since Lori was born, the house was totally silent.

"So tell us what happened already!" Lola finally blurted out.

"Clyde, do you want to tell them or should I?" I said nervously.

"I guess you should do it," Clyde said.

"Oh, Clyde. We're so sorry—" Lori began.

"HE WON!" I shouted, interrupting her.

"WHAT?!" all my sisters yelled at once, jumping up from the couch.

"Clyde won! He got the most votes! He's

going to be the next school treasurer!"

"O-M-gosh! Congratulations!" Leni said.

"It was scientifically improbable, but you beat the odds. Remind me to schedule you for a brain wave study soon," Lisa said as she shook Clyde's hand.

"That's amazing! Congrats!" Luna added.

"Way to dominate, Clydesdale!" Lynn said as she gave Clyde a chest bump.

"I'm sure you were *treasured* by many! *Ha ha ha ha ha!*" Luan said.

"Thanks, everyone!" Clyde said. He smiled wider than I'd ever seen him smile in our whole friendship.

"So how'd you finally beat Chandler?" Lana asked.

"I guess the fact that I actually listened to what the other kids needed helped. I mean, Girl

Jordan is a *huge* Boyz Will Be Boyz fan, and she's never missed Chandler's birthday party. But she told me she loves art club way more, so she voted for me. A lot of kids had stories like that. It was really cool," Clyde said.

"That's great, Clyde," Lori said. "And we're all sorry for getting in your way before."

"Yeah, it sounds like you won by being you," Luna said. "Like you had the thing in the bag the whole time!"

Lola wheeled out Lisa's whiteboard.

"Okay, so now it's time to talk about a game plan for how you're going to do this thing and how you'll get reelected," Lola said.

"Lola," I said.

"Let's talk strategy." She started scribbling on the board with a dry-erase marker. "If Clyde's going to get at least as many votes as this year, he's going to have to start digging up dirt on Chandler now."

"*Lola,*" my sisters said with me.

"But let's really try to focus on what people notice, like smells or sounds," she said, scribbling faster.

"*LOLA!*" we all yelled.

"What?" she asked. I took the marker from her hand and put the cap back on.

"I think it's best if we let Clyde be Clyde."